Cowboy Jesse

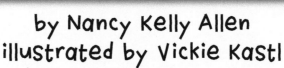

by Nancy Kelly Allen
illustrated by Vickie Kastl

Doodle and Peck Publishing
P.O. Box 852105
Yukon, OK 73085
(405) 354-7422
doodleandpeck@gmail.com

Allen, Nancy Kelly

Cowboy Jesse/ by Allen, Nancy Kelly; illustrated by Vickie L. Kastl

Summary: A young cowboy and a group of aliens become friends after playing hide-and-seek all day. When they leave, the cowboy misses his friends and doesn't think he'll ever see them again. The next day the spaceship returns.

ISBN: 978-1-7337170-9-0 (hard cover) ISBN:978-1-7333462-6-9 (paperback)

1. Cowboys—Fiction 2. Aliens—Fiction 3. Counting—Fiction 4. Friendship—Fiction 5. Illustrator—Vickie L. Kastl

[E]

Library of Congress Control Number:2019946373

"for Bryce"

Nancy Allen

"For my husband, Tom, who suffered through sandwiches three times a day.
To my sons, Doug, Patrick, Court, and Craig who make me proud.
And to my wonderful grandchildren, Cooper, Chloe, Kyla, Kinsley, Owen, and Lucy,
who inspire me.
Also, to my mother whose loving spirit sustains me still."

Vickie Kastl

Simple activities designed to help parents and/or caregivers participate in, and support, a child's literacy skills and educational goals:

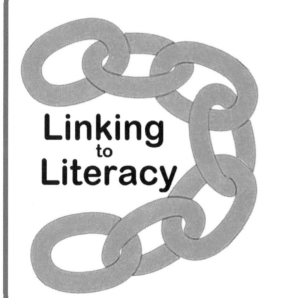

Linking to Literacy

- **Easiest:** Read the story together. Mix up a deck of number cards and help child place them in counting order.

- **More Difficult:** *Write the numbers 1-10, and the number words one through ten, on a piece of paper and cut apart. Mix together. Work together to match the number with its number word.

- **Challenging:** Using cards with number words one through ten, mix them up then work together to place in numerical order.

*Free, printable resources may be found at www.doodleandpeck.com. Click on the Linking to Literacy Resources tab and print off Number Word cards and Number cards.

Jesse saddled his horse and rode west. "Yee-haw! Giddy up!"

ZITTTT! Bloop boop bloop! A spaceship landed in his backyard. One squiggly, wriggly alien flashed his fangs.

Jesse kicked up his cowboy boots and ran behind a tumbleweed. "Whew, I think we're safe now."

Two wierdy, beardy aliens bugged out their eyeballs.

Jesse blinked. He dived into a ditch. "I'm pretty sure we're safe. Lie low."

But three huffing, puffing aliens stirred up a breeze with their funky, skunky burps.

Jesse skedaddled into Old Whiskers' hideout. "Whiskers, you'll keep us safe, right, ol' boy?"

Suddenly four drool-dripping alien tongues shot into the hideout. Yuck!

Jesse wiped the slobber with his bandana and hot-booted over to Lookout Rock. "They'll never find us here."

But five sniffling, snuffling aliens sneezed.

Their drippy noses drizzled snot.

Jesse blocked the snot storm with his bandana and hustled under the prickly cactus. "I'm positive we're safe here."

Jesse watched as six dancing, prancing aliens twirled by.
Rat-a-tap, rat-a-tap.

Jesse bolted around them and hid behind the spaceship. Seven arm-flapping, lip-smacking aliens stomped down the ramp. Jesse climbed up the side of the spaceship. He thought he was safe until...

...eight sneaky, freaky aliens tip-toed toward him.

Jesse climbed higher.

Sunshine sparkled off his spurs.

The aliens squeaked, "Eeeek!" and covered their buggy eyes.

Eeeek!

Eeeek!

Jesse climbed back down. He thought he was safe until...

...out of nowhere, nine bubble-blowing, purple-glowing aliens jumped toward him. But Jesse jumped faster.

Whew! Finally safe. Until...

...ten hopping, bopping aliens leaped and surrounded Jesse. They shuffled closer.

Jesse yanked his lariat and lassoed them. "Whew! Safe at last."

But one by one the aliens slipped out of the rope.

The last alien shuffled over and said, "We came to Earth to find a friend. Will you be our friend?"

Jesse dropped his lasso. "Why didn't you say so? Howdy, pardners!"

Jesse and his new friends tumbled with the tumbleweeds...

skedaddled into Old Whisker's hideout...and hot-booted over to Lookout Rock. But they stayed away from the prickly cactus.

They played all afternoon.

Finally the ten aliens yawned and said goodbye.

Jesse knew he'd probably never see them again. "I miss them already," he thought.

But the next day, as Jesse rode slowly west across the backyard, he heard...ZITTTT! Bloop, boop, bloop!
And Jesse smiled.

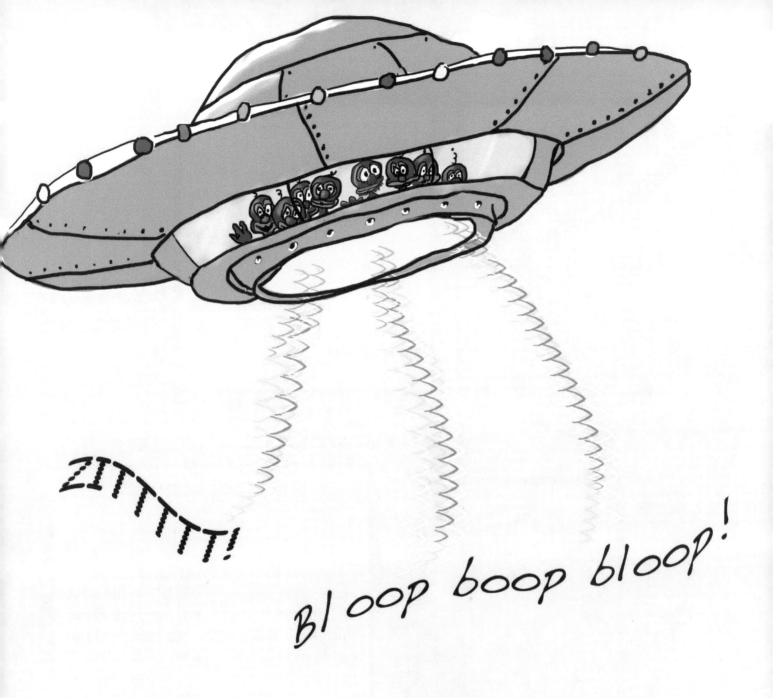

Author, Nancy Kelly Allen

Nancy Kelly Allen is an award-winning author of more than fifty books for children, fiction and nonfiction. She has two master's degrees, Education and Library Science, which led her to teaching children and introducing them to a wide range of literature.

Illustrator, Vickie Kastl

Vickie L. Kastl was born in Central Oklahoma and fell in love with art in second grade. She graduated from UCO with a BA in Education, taught Art and English for thirty-nine years. Vickie has illustrated five children's books. She and her husband travel to collect stories, pictures, and details. She has four sons, five grandchildren and two dogs, Ritchie and Winnie, who pop up in most of her illustrations.